This Book is on FIRE!

By Ron Keres
Artwork by Arthur Lin

GREETINGS, little one!
Finn the Frog here. I am
so glad you came to visit
my book today!

I can't *wait* to show you what I have planned. You are in for a real **TREAT**! Come on. I promise you won't be disappointed!

What do you mean your stomach?!

THAT was you being hungry? Yikes, why didn't you say so? Today your lunch is going to be prepared by the world's most spectacular chef.

Turn the page and let me introduce you to . . . drumroll please . . .

ME!

That's right! I, Finn the Frog, am the chef of your dreams.

The King of the Kitchen.
The Food Fanatic.
The Appetizing Amphibian.

Wait—no . . . scratch that
last one. What I'm trying
to say is: I am very good
at cooking! Now let's get
to it and fix that growly
tummy!

First up: my world-famous pasta.
This is a recipe handed down from
my great-grandfather, Freddie.
He was born in a pond just outside
of Italy.

Quite the chef, that guy! The sauce
is made from **FIRE**-roasted tomatoes.
Oh, I can't wait for you to try this!

Take a bite and tell me that isn't the **BEST** thing you've ever had.

What? No "green stuff?"
You have got to be joking.
I will have you know
that "green stuff" is
organic **lily pad**, imported
all the way from Italy!
It's a delicacy!

That lily pad was **EXPENSIVE** and now it's getting washed down the sink. **Rude.** *That's what it is.* Would it be so hard to say, "The green stuff's not my favorite"?

Never mind. Just wait until you see what I have planned next! Get ready for your taste buds to do a happy dance!

I have two words for you: **MEAT. LOAF.**
This isn't your grannie's meat loaf.
Ha! It's MY grannie's actually—but
with my own special **FLARE**.

Good ol' American comfort food.
So tender. So juicy. Simply the best.
I bet you'll be licking your plate
clean after this one!

I'll have you know that **mush** comes from the finest SWAMP MUD this side of the Mississippi! You sure are hard to please. Wait! I know what you'll like!

This next dish is—without question—the **BEST** one I make.
Ahhh. Do you smell it? HEAVENLY!

Specially marinated and **FLAME** grilled Brazilian Ribeye with whipped potatoes. Consider yourself *lucky*, kid. This dish is *delicioso!*

STINKY? That's preposterous!
Everyone knows that soaking the
meat in **POND WATER** is the
best way to tenderize it—
and it provides a lovely aroma.

Well, every time *I* soak in it,
it softens me right up and *I*
think *I* smell fabulous!

WHAT DID YOU SAY?! No, frog legs are **NOT** on the menu! Oh, boy. This is a disaster! I should have just made you those little dinosaur nuggets. Or noodles and butter. Or grilled cheese. Or . . .

I know I'm a great chef—
and you're a hungry kid,
so grilled cheese it is.

Basic. Bland. **BORING!**
No special skills required
to cook this one.

Oh, what difference does it make?
I've already made so many dirty
dishes, what's one more. I'd better
get started on them. You know how
I feel about a mess, and cleaning
this one up is going to take me all—

ACK! I got distracted and forgot to flip your grilled cheese. And look—now it's burning!

Don't panic, Finn. Don't panic. You can handle this.

No you **CAN'T**. Mayday! Mayday!
This book is . . . **ON**

Sorry about the sandwich.
Let me make you a new one.

Huh?? You're taking that?!
Why? What are you thinking!?
You don't have to do that just
to be polite.

Ohh! Slightly burnt grilled cheese is your favorite?

Maybe you're **NOT** impossible to please! I guess I never thought of asking what **YOU** like. I just assumed everyone would like my food.

I shall call it . . .

TOTALLY TOASTED CHEESY PLEASEY!

WHOA. Why is my book shaking **AGAIN?!**

Is this another earthqua—

BUUU

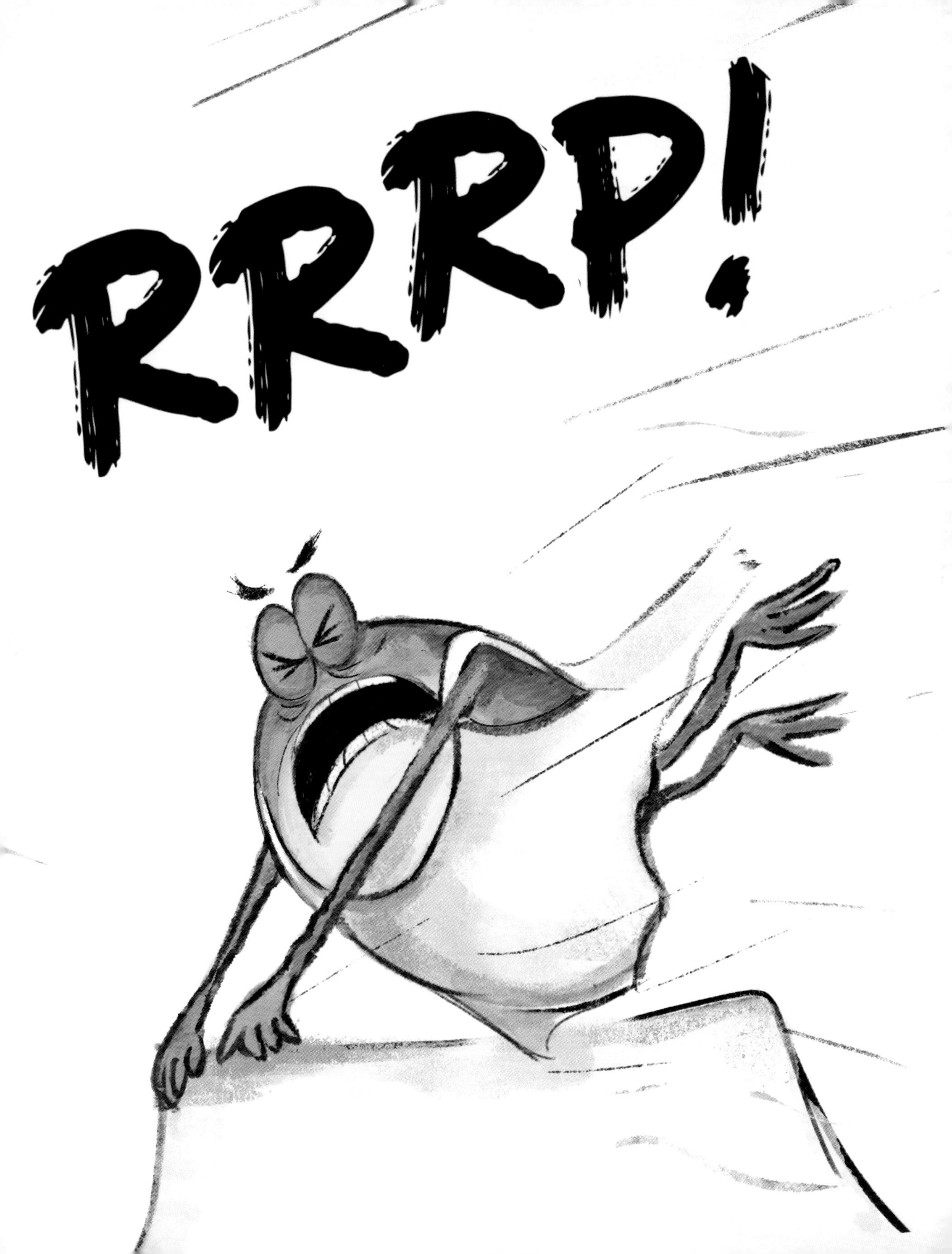
RRRP!

WOW.

You know, in many cultures, a burp is considered a compliment to the chef . . .

I'll take it!

Ooo, look. You're not the
only one who likes burned
grilled cheese. Maybe mistakes
aren't always a bad thing!

Care for some dessert?

This Book Is On Fire!

For permission requests contact:
rkbookpermissions@gmail.com

ISBN: 979-8-9859112-8-2
Printed in China
13 12 11 10 9 8 7 6 5 4 3

Illustrations by Arthur Lin, arteelin.com
Published by Buzzbook Press

BUZZBOOK
PRESS

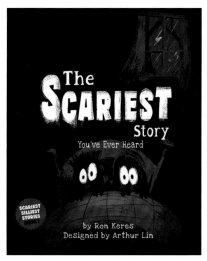

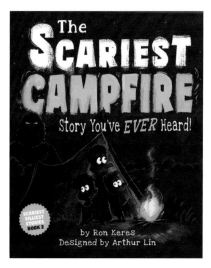

For a free how-to-draw Finn the Frog tutorial and printable coloring sheets, go to ronkeres.com or scan the code with your device.

Enjoyed this book? Please leave a review!